To order additional copies of this book, contact:
Xlibris LLC
1-888-795-4274
www.Xlibris.com
Orders@Xlibris.com

Printed in Canada by Friesens
Altona, Canada
December, 2013
91151

for Danny and Nathan

Here told is the story of an angel so small,

who was only but 4 years old.

He followed the path of the blessed light,

to finally find heaven to hold.

There he would play and play,

he would play all day.

But his most favorite thing of all,

was to play with his little treasure box

that he took with him when the Lord called.

There was a Butterfly with wings of gold,

and a piece of a branch that was very old.

Add two special stones that he found

in some stuff,

and the very old collar from his

loving dog Fluff.

Then all of a sudden the word went about,
that the angels gathered round to hear.

A great event was to happen that night,
the newborn king was about to appear.

So as the angels brought out their special
gifts, the tiniest angel sat in awe.

So he hurried and got
his treasured box,
and laid it
down low in
the straw.

Then the tiniest angel ran away and cried,

his gift was too modest he saw.

That Butterfly with wings of gold,

the piece of a branch that was very old.

Those two special stones that he found in

some stuff,

and the very old collar from his

loving dog Fluff.

But the Lord decided to pick this box,

which was blessed by the love of a child.

And all of a sudden it started to glow,

and stood out from all the gifts piled.

Then the little box began to rise up,
and from inside came a bright light...

It rose high in the sky and became the
Lord's star,
and today the box still glows bright.

So when you go at night and stand under
the sky,
and look at the stars far and wide. . .

you will know that the happiest angel of
them all,
is the tiniest angel with pride.

⸺⸎⸎⸎⸺

The Butterfly with wings of gold,
the piece of a branch that was very old.
Two special stones that he found
in some stuff,
and the very old collar from his loving dog
Fluff.

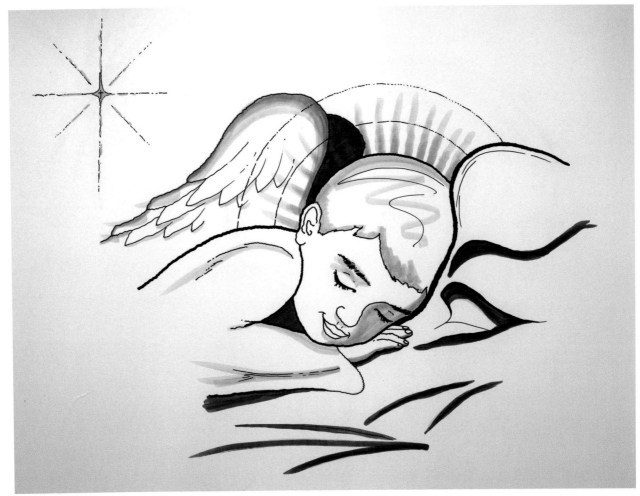